DISNEY·PIXAR

# THE INCREDIBLES

## DASH TO THE RESCUE

ADVANCE PUBLISHERS

Dash Parr was the fastest boy in the world. He belonged to a family of superheroes. His mom, Helen, could stretch into any shape. His dad, Bob, was superstrong. Dash's sister, Violet, created force fields and turned invisible. Only the baby, Jack-Jack didn't seem to have any superpowers.

But the government had told the Supers not to use their powers. So Dash's parents wouldn't let him show off his speed. Sometimes Dash felt so frustrated he just had to let off steam! Today he had run to his teacher's chair and put a tack on it. He was so fast even the teacher's video camera didn't record him.

"We need to find you a more constructive outlet," his mom said as she drove Dash home from the school principal's office.

"Let me go out for sports," Dash said for the zillionth time.

His mom shook her head. "You are incredibly competitive and a bit of a show-off. Right now the world wants us to fit in."

Dash didn't want to fit in. He wanted to show the world how fast he was.

That night at dinner, Dash told his dad about what happened in school.
"Wow!" Bob exclaimed. "You were bookin'!"
"Bob, we are not encouraging this," Helen said.
Bob stormed from the table. Like Dash, Bob was frustrated that he couldn't use his superpowers.

Dash looked at Violet slumped in her chair and decided to do his favorite thing after running—tease her about her crush on a boy at school.

"Shut up, you little insect!" Violet shouted. She lunged for Dash, but he raced around the table. Violet threw a force field, and Dash slammed into it. Plates and cups crashed to the floor.

"Dash! Violet! Stop it!" Helen stretched her arms and held the flailing children apart. "Bob! Do something!" She shouted. Bob stomped from his den and hoisted the table into the air—with everyone dangling from it. It was another typical dinner at the Parr residence.

When your kids have incredible Super powers, sometimes the only way to keep control is to use your own! When Dash and Violet fight, things can soon get out of hand—unless that hand is Super stretchy and belongs to Helen Parr!

For a few days, Dash tried to behave like an average boy. But it was hard. All he could think about was running. Then something exciting happened. His mom came home with some cool-looking Super suits.

"Hey are those for us?" Dash shouted. Before Helen could stop him, Dash grabbed his Super suit and zoomed off. Seconds later he ran back into her bedroom wearing it.

Dash is one of the fastest things on Earth. Competitive, a bit of a show-off, and full of restless energy, he often drives his family to distraction! Dash wishes he didn't have to keep his Super speediness a secret—he's not even allowed to play sports at school in case anyone suspects his Super nature.

"Look! I'm The Dash!" he exclaimed. Helen pushed him out of the bedroom and shut the door. Dash thrust Violet's suit at her.

"What makes you think it's special?" Violet asked, holding hers up.

"I dunno," Dash answered with a shrug. "Why'd Mom try to hide it?"

Helen hurried out, carrying a travel bag. "I should be back tonight, late," she said as she left.

*What was going on?* Dash wondered. Violet was curious, too. She called a babysitter for Jack-Jack, then she and Dash followed Helen to the airport and sneaked on board the jet.

Dash crouched behind a seat, hardly able to contain his excitement! He had the coolest Super suit ever, and he was going on an adventure! This was turning out to be the most awesome day of his entire life.

Then his mom discovered him and Violet. She was furious.

"It's not my fault. And Dash ran away." Violet started.

"That's not true!" Dash interrupted her.

BEEEEEEP! A warning signal shrilled from the cockpit.

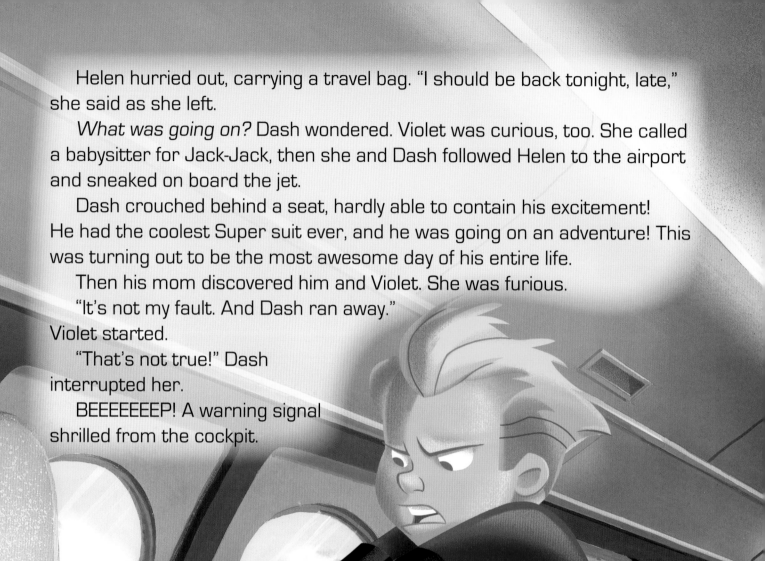

Violet is a very cool and clever kid—but she just doesn't believe in herself. She's so busy trying to be normal that she never gives herself a chance to shine. But when she's forced to fight with her family, that chance finally comes—and Violet gains the confidence she's always lacked.

Missiles streaked toward the jet. Helen sent the jet into a deep dive, but there was no escaping the missiles.

"Abort!" Helen yelled, shoving Dash and Violet from the jet as it exploded in a fiery ball.

Dash plummeted downward. The air whistled past his ears. The ocean rushed upward.

"Mom!" Dash screamed. Then he felt her arms around him. Holding her children, Helen shaped herself into a parachute and they splashed down. Dash struggled to keep his head above the churning waves. Suddenly the "awesome" adventure wasn't exciting—it was scary.

"We're dead. We're dead!" He spluttered and coughed.

"Get a grip or I will ground you for a month—understand?" Helen snapped. "Trust me." She pointed toward shore. They could reach it—if they worked together.

Helen stretched herself into a raft, and Dash kicked so fast his legs blurred. The raft churned through the waves, leaving a streak of white foam behind.

When they reached shore, Dash crawled onto the beach. His legs felt like floppy rubber bands.

"What a trooper," his mom smiled at him. "I'm so proud of you."

"Thanks, Mom." Dash replied. A warm glow filled him. He had used his super speed to help save his mom and sister. Suddenly he felt proud, too.

Super-elastic Elastigirl can bend, stretch, or twist herself into any shape. She can flatten herself as well as form a human parachute to slow someone's fall. Elastigirl can elongate her body, within a surprising limit, to become as long as she needs to be for any given situation.

That night, Dash and Violet sat by a small campfire at the mouth of a cave listening to their mom. She was going to look for their dad.

"Use your powers," she told them. "I'm counting on you. Be strong. Dash, if anything goes wrong, I want you to run as fast as you can."

"As fast as I can?" Dash asked. His eyes gleamed with excitement. This was a first! His mom had always told him to hide his speed.

"I'll be back by morning," Helen said. She disappeared into the darkness. Violet and Dash were on their own.

Helen leaves the children alone on Nomanisan, putting Violet in charge while she looks for Bob. The young Super is afraid—she knows the bad guys won't take pity on them just because they're kids. She practices her powers and slowly begins to gain confidence in herself.

Dash fidgeted by the fire while Violet practiced making force fields. He was bored, so he decided to look around.

"Mom said to stay hidden." Violet reminded him.

Dash made a face. Big sisters are so bossy! "I'm not gonna leave the cave," he answered.

Dash wandered through the cave until he came to the edge of a deep tunnel. A red light glowed at the far end. It seemed to be getting bigger. It wasn't a light. It was a wall of flame roaring through the tunnel straight at him and Violet.

Under the surface of Nomanisan, there is a maze of metal corridors that stretches over several miles. Every part of the base can be accessed by this network of tunnels. There are advanced security measures to thwart intruders, such as being able to access rooms only with special keycards.

"Ahhhh!" Screaming, Dash raced to Vi and pulled her from the cave. Seconds later flames erupted from the cave's mouth. In the distance, an enormous rocket blasted into the sky.

"What did you DO?" Violet asked. Dash just shook his head.

*This place is beyond weird*, he thought.

Dash didn't know that the island was the home of Syndrome, his dad's worst enemy, or that the island was covered with security alerts. But he and Violet found out the next morning when they triggered an alarm. Suddenly, menacing guards in strange-looking Velocipods surrounded them.

"Dash! Run!" Violet shouted. Then she vanished.

Dash bolted. The Velocipods were fast, but he was faster. Dash tore through the jungle. He swung on vines, rocketed off cliffs, and zoomed through tunnels. His legs churned so fast he ran across water without sinking.

"Whooooo-aaa!" Dash shouted as he ran. He felt awesome, amazing, fantastic! If it weren't for the guards, this would be FUN! Just then he slammed into a guard who was trying to catch Vi.

"Don't touch my sister!" Dash yelled. Violet could be a pain sometimes, but she was his sister—and no one else was allowed to bother her!

Violet threw a force field around herself and Dash. Dash propelled it like a hamster in a ball. They spun through the jungle faster and faster. Then WHUMP! The ball smacked into Helen and Bob. They had heard the alarm and had run to save their children.

Dash had never been so glad to see his parents. But as they hugged each other, velocipods exploded from the jungle. Helen and Bob went into action. Helen coiled, stretched, and snapped scissor kicks. Bob chopped, smashed, slammed Velocipods into the trees, and knocked guards out.

Dash had never seen his parents use their super powers as a team. It was awesome.

Unfortunately, it wasn't awesome enough.

Syndrome's guards are a highly trained crack combat unit ready to counter any possible threat. The thuggish brutes are armed and extremely dangerous. Anyone setting foot on the island of Nomanisan does so at their own risk.

Suddenly, Syndrome stepped out from the jungle. In a few minutes he had imprisoned Dash and his family in his electrical handcuffs. Syndrome planned to unleash his battle robot, the Omnidroid, on Municiburg. Nothing could stop him. Being superfast couldn't help Dash or his family now.

But Violet had used a force field to break free of the handcuffs. When Syndrome left, she released her family. They were back in action! Even Dash had to admit that Violet had done something pretty cool.

Soon, the family was blasting toward Municiburg in a van that Helen was holding from a rocket.

When the city came into sight, Helen let go and climbed into the van. The van slammed onto the highway, swerved, screeched, rocked, and rolled to a stop.

Dash laughed. "Let's do that again!" He exclaimed.

It's while trapped on Nomanisan that the Incredible family find themselves fighting together for the first time. They soon show Syndrome's guards that together they're a force to be reckoned with!

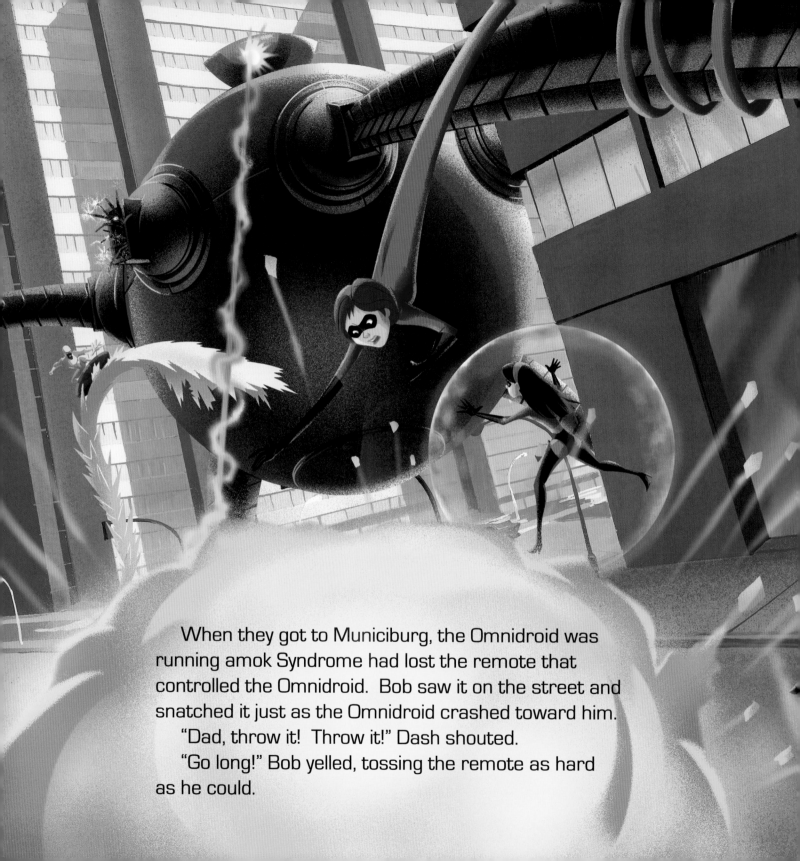

When they got to Municiburg, the Omnidroid was
running amok Syndrome had lost the remote that
controlled the Omnidroid.  Bob saw it on the street and
snatched it just as the Omnidroid crashed toward him.

"Dad, throw it!  Throw it!" Dash shouted.

"Go long!" Bob yelled, tossing the remote as hard
as he could.

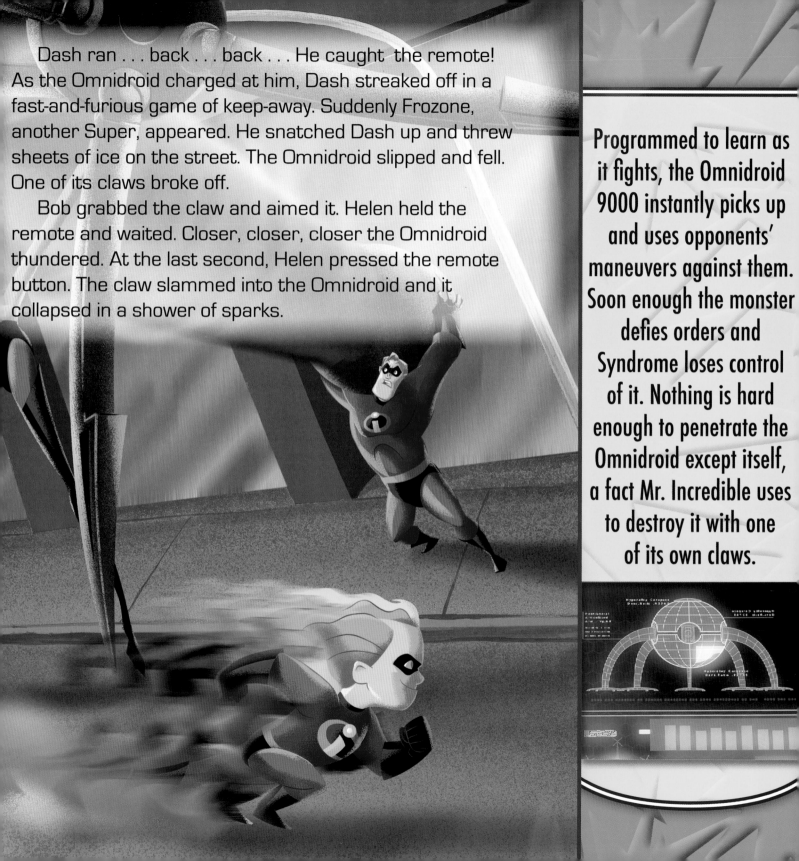

Dash ran . . . back . . . back . . . He caught the remote! As the Omnidroid charged at him, Dash streaked off in a fast-and-furious game of keep-away. Suddenly Frozone, another Super, appeared. He snatched Dash up and threw sheets of ice on the street. The Omnidroid slipped and fell. One of its claws broke off.

Bob grabbed the claw and aimed it. Helen held the remote and waited. Closer, closer, closer the Omnidroid thundered. At the last second, Helen pressed the remote button. The claw slammed into the Omnidroid and it collapsed in a shower of sparks.

Programmed to learn as it fights, the Omnidroid 9000 instantly picks up and uses opponents' maneuvers against them. Soon enough the monster defies orders and Syndrome loses control of it. Nothing is hard enough to penetrate the Omnidroid except itself, a fact Mr. Incredible uses to destroy it with one of its own claws.

They had beaten the Omnidroid! And Dash's super speed had helped his family win. He looked at the cheering crowds gathering around and grinned. For the first time, Dash felt like a real—true—superhero! In fact—he felt INCREDIBLE!

"That was the best vacation ever!" Dash exclaimed. "I love our family!"

After their victory over the Omnidroid, Dash's mom and dad decided to let him play sports. On one warm, sunny day, Dash pounded down the track at his first track meet while his family cheered in the stands.

Dash made himself finish second, but he didn't care. He didn't have to be in first place to feel like a winner. He knew his superpowers would always be there for him when he needed them. Just like his incredible family.

No sooner do the Incredibles bring down the Omnidroid than the Underminer bursts through the streets with his enormous drilling machine. The molelike monster declares war on peace and happiness, but the Incredibles aren't worried. There's nothing they love more than a new challenge.

# JOKES, RIDDLES, AND SILLY STUFF!

## ... VOLUME 1 ANSWERS!

WHY ARE
SUPERHEROES SO COOL?
BECAUSE THEY
HAVE SO MANY FANS.

WHAT HAPPENS TO
SYNDROME'S JET WHEN IT
SITS OUT IN THE RAIN?
IT GETS WET.

HEADLINES YOU'LL NEVER SEE:
EDNA MODE DESIGNS
SUPERSUIT WITH TWO CAPES!
DASH PARR WINS THIRD PLACE!
VIOLET PARR TALKS TO BOYS!
ELASTIGIRL SNAPS AT CHILDREN!

HOW FAST IS DASH?
HE'S SO FAST,
THE CHEETAHS IN THE
STANDS WERE IMPRESSED!

HOW COOL IS FROZONE?
HE'S SO COOL,
ICE CUBES GET JEALOUS.

HOW FAST IS DASH?
HE'S SO FAST, HE GOT A
SPEEDING TICKET ON THE
HIGHWAY WITHOUT A CAR!

HOW MANY OMNIDROIDS
DOES IT TAKE TO SCREW
IN A LIGHT BULB?
SILLY HUMAN. OMNIDROIDS
CAN SEE WITHOUT LIGHT.

WHAT DID
EDNA MODE'S
LICENSE PLATE
(NO C&PS) SAY?
NO CAPES!

WHAT DO YOU FIND IN A
SUPERHERO'S BATHROOM?
A SUPERBOWL.

WHAT IS A SUPERHERO'S
FAVORITE PART OF THE JOKE?
THE PUNCH LINE!

DASH IS IN A RACE.
HE RUNS BY THE PERSON
IN SECOND PLACE.
WHAT PLACE IS HE IN?
SECOND.

UNSCRAMBLE THE NAMES
OF BUDDY PINE'S WEAPONS:
ODDINIMOR: OMNIDROID
OMBRYIMIA: IMMOBIRAY

WHO ELSE WAS IN
MR. INCREDIBLE'S
SUPERHERO GRADUATING CLASS?
HUGH R STRONG
MARV ELLIS
ANITA HAND
WILLY HELP
BEA BRAVE
BD BEST

WHAT'S A VILLAIN'S
FAVORITE SOUP?
SCREAM OF TOMATO.

MORE HEADLINES
YOU'LL NEVER SEE:
FROZONE RETIRES;
BURNED OUT LOUD
EXPLOSION DOWNTOWN;
NO SUPERHEROES SHOW
BUDDY PINE DEBUTS
NEW ROBOTIC PIZZA
DELIVERY SERVICE

[DASH]
WHAT'S THE DIFFERENCE
BETWEEN HERE—ZIP—AND THERE?
THE LETTER T.

[EDNA MODE]
DID YOU HEAR ABOUT THE
MAN WHO PUT ON A PAIR OF
CLEAN SOCKS EVERY DAY?
BY THE END OF
THE WEEK HE
COULDN'T GET HIS
SHOES ON.

HOW FASHIONABLE
IS EDNA MODE?
SHE'S SO FASHIONABLE,
PLAIDS AND CHECKS
STAY APART WHEN
SHE'S AROUND.

HOW FAST IS DASH?
HE'S SO FAST, HE ONCE
CAUGHT HIS OWN PASS!

HOW STRONG IS
MR. INCREDIBLE?
HE'S SO STRONG, HE
PITCHES HORSESHOES
WITHOUT TAKING THEM
OFF THE HORSES!

BUMPER STICKER ON
THE INCREDIMOBILE:
BABY ON BOARD

WHY DID THE OMNIDROID
CROSS THE ROAD?
TO GET A BYTE TO EAT.

HOW COOL IS FROZONE?
HE'S SO COOL, HE
AIR-CONDITIONED
THE SAHARA DESERT.